Taken by Two Cops

Taken, Volume 13

Jasmine Black

Published by Spunky Girl Publishing, 2022.

Also by Jasmine Black

Standalone
Shared Boxed Set

Taken by Two Cops

Jasmine Black

Twenty-four-year-old police officer Martina "Marty" Webster gets a fascinating opportunity to go undercover as a lady of the evening in order to catch a criminal. She's thrilled to be partnered with the two older hunky cops she's secretly attracted to. The male officers are going to teach her all she needs to know to carry out her assignment and they're going to leave no holes barred...

Other stories by Jasmine Black include:

Taken by Two Doctors, Taken by Three Doctors, Taken by Two Bikers, Taken by Three Bikers, Taken by Two Billionaires, Taken by Three Billionaires, Taken by Two Bosses, Taken by Two Cowboys, Taken by Three Cowboys, Taken by Two Firefighters, Taken by Two Carpenters, Taken by Two Personal Trainers, Taken by Two Santas, Taken by Two Elves, Taken by Three Bodyguards, Taken by Two Cops, Taken by Two Prison Guards, Taken by Two Lifeguards, Taken by Two Mountain Men and more!

Copyright

Author Note

Chapter One

"**O**fficer Webster! In my office!" My boss, Lt. Stryker called out the instant I entered the precinct locker room. He impatiently waved for me to hurry and then he disappeared from the doorway he'd been standing in.

I tensed as several of my male colleagues, who were in various stages of undress, snickered and made low ooooh sounds. I flipped them my middle finger and received a volley of laughter.

I couldn't help but smile and shake my head as I opened my locker, tossed in my purse, hung up my sweater, shut the door and flipped my middle finger to them on my way out. There came another chorus of laughter.

I was glad *they* were happy. Me, on the other hand, felt very tense.

As I approached the lieutenant's office, nervous perspiration popped out on my palms.

There were usually two reasons why one of us got summoned to the boss's office. One reason was to be reprimanded for doing something wrong and I could not for the life of me think of where I had screwed up. The other reason, he was giving me an assignment.

I prayed it was the latter as it beat patrolling the streets in uniform.

His door was closed, so I knocked lightly. He instructed me to enter, and when I did, I halted in the doorway.

Two senior undercover officers were already seated there. I sighed in relief. This was good news. I was going to get an assignment!

"Come on in, Marty. Close the door behind you. Take a seat," Lieutenant Stryker said.

I nodded, acted cool and professional, and sat down between Curtis and Bill. Just being this near to both of these men made my breath halt and my pussy tremble with need. I had the hots for both of them.

In my opinion, they were the best-looking cops in the precinct, and I'd heard through the grapevine that both men had recently been dumped by the girlfriend they shared.

I worshipped them from afar. They were older than me. I was twenty-four and they were twenty-eight. I loved that they were roque in that they wore their hair really long. Curtis' straight chestnut-colored hair went way past his shoulders, like that Fabio character that was on my grandmother's romance book covers. Curtis had a neatly cropped beard and moustache, which I found sexy. His eyes were deep brown and reminded me of dark chocolate fudge.

His partner, Bill, was just as hunky. His hair was a lighter brown and he had the palest blue eyes that kind of looked through you. They reminded me of azure crystal. I'd caught him watching me on several occasions and I'd secretly hoped they would ask me out. I'd never been with two guys at the same time and I found the idea intriguing.

"Okay, we're all here. What do you have for us, Lieutenant??" Curtis asked.

Lieutenant Stryker sighed and pursed his lips. He was an older man, balding, overweight and he always looked tired.

"I don't like dropping this assignment on you this way. However, all the more experienced undercover officers are swamped with their assignments. I believe you and Bill have experience for this job but Marty may need some training in this regard and she's here because she is our only available woman officer."

He let the last two words dangle.

Oh. Oh. I sensed this assignment might not be the best for me, especially because he'd said I was the only available woman. That probably meant I would be some sort of bait for a man.

"Don't give me that scrunched-up face, officer," The lieutenant said as he stared me down until I felt the size of a pea.

Then he smiled like he was pleased with himself in lording it over me.

What an asshole.

"If you like, you can give me that face when you have all the facts," he added.

Double asshole.

He turned his attention to Curtis.

"And you, no rolling your eyes, Officer Stanco."

I smiled inwardly. It appeared Curtis was not impressed with the Lieutenant either.

Curtis remained silent and the lieutenant nodded his satisfaction.

"Good, now that I have your undivided attention. What I was saying earlier. Everyone is swamped with their assignments. And since you three are available, then you might be interested in catching Crazy Horse."

I visibly tensed at the familiar name. I noticed Curtis and Bill were stiffening as well.

"Crazy Horse, the pimp? I thought he was in prison?" I asked.

The lieutenant nodded.

"He was. He got out early for good behaviour. He's been out a week. Word on the street is he is wanting to buy women from other pimps because while he was in prison, another local pimp took his ladies and he won't give the ladies back. Crazy Horse wants women that are already in the sex trade, so he can get the money he needs to start grooming new ones. If we can catch him making a deal in buying one, we can get him off the streets again. That's why you're here, Marty. I want you to be that woman he wants to buy. The woman who will take him down."

Surprise washed over me and I heard Bill whistle lowly and Curtis swore softly beneath his breath.

This was a huge assignment for me. I've been working toward detective status but I wasn't an expert on the sex trade or on how to be a hooker. I decided to keep playing it cool and just ask questions.

"I was new here when Crazy Horse was put away. He's the violent one? The one who brands his women with the letters CH on their backside?" I asked.

"That's him. The letter C on one ass cheek and the letter H on the other. Right after the branding he expects them to work," the lieutenant said.

I winced as I imagined how much pain one went through after being branded and then having to have sex right after.

"I heard that affection and violence are how Crazy Horse keeps his women trauma bonded to him," Curtis said.

The lieutenant nodded and continued the conversation.

"He picks vulnerable females. Usually runaways, the homeless, the desperate or a female in a domestic violence situation. Crazy Horse treats his victim really nice at the beginning. He gives her nice clothes. A nice apartment. Takes care of her and makes her feel protected and safe. He also isolates her. Takes away any support system she might have and pretends he really cares for her. When she is hooked to his great charming ways, he slowly changes and starts to be controlling. Then the violence starts and he blames her for being the cause of his irritation. She's guilt tripped into feeling she has done something wrong and she tries to please him. A pattern starts. He's Mr. Nice Guy for awhile again, then he gets pissed off at her for some other reason. She tries to please him some more. The cycle continues until the woman will do anything to gratify him. Eventually, Crazy Horse adds her to his stable of prostitutes."

My boss's face grew dire as he stared at me and his expression sent shivers of dread up my spine.

"You will literally have to be a hooker, Marty. You'll have to make it believable. Crazy Horse will want to see you have sex with your pimp. In your case, two pimps, which will be Curtis and Bill."

Geez. Yeah, sure I had the hots for both Curtis and Bill, but this was a crazy way to get sex.

"And he will want to try you out before buying you. He likes to sample the goods. He knows what to say too to avoid being arrested, so until he's satisfied you aren't cops, he'll be very careful with his words. So you'll have your work cut out for you. If you take this assignment and we get him off the streets, you'll have saved countless young women from getting trapped into servitude with this guy," he said.

I nodded. I appreciated that I would be helping women from falling prey to this predator. But having sex with Curtis and Bill *and* Crazy Horse. Seriously?

"I'm not liking the idea of her having sex with him," Curtis protested.

Well, hallelujah. Neither am I!

"If you all can figure out a way to take him down before he samples her, then by all means do it. But just remember this. We've got one shot at this guy. If he gets suspicious, he'll walk. That's it. Game over. He will go underground at some other unsuspecting city and continue to do his nasty deeds."

The Lieutenant looked straight at me.

"I'm going to need an answer from all of you pretty much right away. And, Marty, just so you know, this will go down on your record toward your detective status."

I sighed.

"And if I say no?"

"Either way, your answer will be a matter of record."

Shit! I had been working toward being a detective for long time now. My two older brothers and my dad were detectives. If I turned down this assignment, and the authorities who decide if I were detective material would think I was a wimp and they'd pass on me. On the other hand, having sex with Curtis and Bill made me feel quite hot and bothered. The challenge of this assignment was starting to excite me.

"I'm in," Curtis said softly.

"I am too," Bill replied.

The three men looked at me awaiting my answer.

Tingles of excitement pushed away my dread. I liked a challenge. Always had. And if Curtis and Bill weren't afraid to have sex, then why should I?

"Gentlemen, count me in." I answered.

Chapter Two

"We're going to need some butt plugs for you, Marty." Bill said. I almost swallowed the wrong way on the tequila I was sipping. It was several hours after this morning's meeting and we'd met after lunch for drinks at a local bar, with the idea to strategize how we would get Crazy Horse interested in taking a look at me.

We weren't wasting time with this assignment. It hadn't even been an hour after all of us agreed to work together that the Lieutenant had secured a budget for us to use. I'd immediately gone shopping for some sexy dresses, one of which I was wearing now.

It was a chic black mini dress. Well, actually a mini skirt and a black bra and the rest of the dress was transparent mesh exposing my mid-section and belly button. I'd also curled my usually straight blonde mid-back length hair, splashed on some heavy-duty makeup and then met up with Curtis and Bill here.

I found it quite exciting that the two men couldn't keep their eyes off me and I loved the scorching way they watched me like I was some kind of a feast, ready to be devoured.

"Yeah, definitely butt plugs. Unless..." Curtis said thoughtfully.

He looked at me with a weird kind of expression. I thought his cheeks were a bit flushed, but that could be the beer hitting him.

"Unless what? I asked, not understanding what Curtis was getting at.

Bill leaned forward and gently placed his palm over the back of my hand. Electric heat zipped through me at his touch.

"No offence intended, but what Curtis and I need to know is if you are anally active. We won't need plugs to prepare you if you're already actively having anal sex. And we need to know if you're a virgin. In other words how much experience do you have?"

Oh, my goodness. My face and neck were warming up. I forced my embarrassment away. I was a cop on a mission. I realized that intimate details were needed for this assignment to work, yet their blistering, interested gazes made me wonder if the questions might also be personal.

I stared at Curtis, forcing myself to hold eye contact. I certainly didn't want them to think I was a prude.

"I am not a virgin. I have been with two guys. However, no, I have never had anal sex and my experience is limited. They call it vanilla sex if I'm remembering right."

Curtis nodded, grabbed his frosted mug of beer, and took a few swallows as he watched me with those hot brown eyes. He seemed satisfied with my answer.

"And what about you two? Have you guys ever had anal sex?"

Hey, if they could ask me that question, then I could ask them. I smiled inwardly as both men shifted uncomfortably in their chairs.

Bill's blue eyes concentrated on his beer and to my surprise, he nodded.

Holy shit, Really? I wondered whom he had had anal sex with. Maybe Curtis? I didn't ask. That was getting too personal.

I peered at Curtis who shook his head.

Okay, so one of them had had anal. So what? I just wanted them to feel uncomfortable with the question, like I had been. Mission accomplished.

"I'll swing by an adult store and pick up some plugs and other items on my way home," Bill said.

Curtis nodded.

Bill kept his scorching gaze on me and his palm stayed on my hot hand. I felt feverish and my pussy grew warm and wet as I wondered what other items he had in mind for me.

He continued to stare at me as he spoke.

"If you two want to drop by my place around seven tonight, we can get Marty outfitted with the small plug. Getting you anally prepared will take a few days, depending on how comfortable you are with them. We will need you to be able to accommodate a generous size penis back there."

Oh boy, a generous sized penis.

I creamed harder.

"She'll need to wear a wire too. So everything gets recorded," Curtis said.

"Kind of hard to wear a wire if we're having sex in front of Crazy Horse with no clothes on," I reminded them. I wasn't even sure I could do something like that in front of a stranger if it came to that.

Curtis chuckled.

"That's where Bill and my experience come in. You'll be outfitted with nipple clamps, labia clamps, slave apparatus...the works. We can get a high-tech wire into one of the clamps."

"Wow, really," I commented. The mention of slave apparatus had my body humming.

"No worries, Marty. We will take good care of you," Curtis whispered in soft voice.

Bill squeezed my hand. I wasn't sure if it was a reassurance gesture or maybe he was hitting on me?

"Curtis is right. We will protect you. But we're going to have to practice being intimate. We're going to have to be quite at ease with each other, so Crazy Horse doesn't get suspicious."

I nodded, feeling my pussy *and* my ass tremble as I imagined having sex with these two guys.

"Okay, when do we start?" I asked them. I held my breath as I eagerly awaited an answer.

"We'll start some training, tonight," Bill answered.

I STOPPED IN FRONT of Room 3001, slipped my hand into my purse and brought out my compact. I flipped it open and checked to make sure everything was in order. After drinks at the bar, the three of us had parted ways and I'd gone back home to have a shower, change into another sexy dress, grab some supper and then come here.

Thankfully my makeup looked great. I'd put on fresh makeup after my shower and gave my hair another round of curls with the curling iron. I looked hot. Like a hooker. Maybe even better than one. I reset some dangling wisps of hair and then I smiled at my reflection in the tiny compact mirror.

I nodded and blew out a tense breath. Okay, I was good to go.

After getting rid of the compact, I knocked.

I felt tense as Bill opened his apartment door and ushered me inside.

"Glad you could make it," he said as he closed the door and faced me. He looked hot. A five o'clock shadow had formed on his cheeks and chin. I always found bristle on a man's face quite attractive. His eyes sparkled with appreciation as he eyed me from head-to-toe. I did the same to him.

He wore a well-fitting beige Ralph Lauren polo shirt which illuminated his wide shoulders and large expanse of a chest. Jeans and bare feet were the rest of his attire. Then I gazed back at his face to find a cute furrow between his brows.

"You look surprised that I'm here. Did you think I'd back out?" I asked, checking him for a reaction.

He chuckled but said nothing as he motioned me to follow him.

To tell the truth, the thought of cancelling this gig did cross my mind. But having that black mark on my record in refusing an assignment spurned me to go through with this hooker act. The two men had said they'd protect me and figure out a way of getting me out of having sex with Crazy Horse. I trusted them. They were fellow cops. They had my back.

And I had to admit that having sex with both men was a bonus. A huge bonus.

As I entered Bill's living room, I was impressed with his place. I'd never been here and from what I was seeing so far, it looked quite nice.

It was modern and open concept. The kitchen, dining room, living room and office were all one huge room. There were plenty of windows. The walls were painted a pristine white, the furniture was all black, the décor in dark chocolate brown and coffee milk shades and the carpeting a luxurious plush white.

"Well, it will take more than sex to frighten me away," I teased as I peered out his living room window. I got a funny feeling in the pit of my tummy as I gazed down at the ant-like people and tiny cars that were directly below on the street.

"And it's a good thing I'm not afraid of heights," I murmured.

We were on the thirtieth floor and everywhere I looked I saw rooftops of other buildings and not too far in the distance there were towering apartment buildings, even higher than this one. But those buildings didn't obscure the view. There was a magnificent sunset of gold, gray and pink tinged clouds that billowed over the glistening waters of the New York harbor. In the distance, I could barely make out the Statue of Liberty on the horizon.

"Nice view too," I complimented as I turned away and spied him bending over, peering into his fridge, giving me a nice sample of jean clad curvy butt cheeks.

"It's home," Bill answered with a shrug, not realizing I'd complimented his ass and not the skyline.

"So, Marty? Did you grab a bite to eat? If not, I can whip you up something. I make a pretty mean spicy Indian masala omelette frittata and a cold mango milkshake."

"The man cooks?" I asked.

From the angle I stood, I caught his grin.

"You sound surprised. I cook spicy hot out of the bedroom and in the bedroom," he replied, without looking up.

I trembled at his confident words. I couldn't wait to see how good he cooked in the sex department.

"Good to know and yes, I ate a salad." I answered.

He nodded and shut the fridge door, moving further into his kitchen to a water cooler set in a corner.

"Want a glass of water?" he asked as he served himself.

"Maybe later, and maybe later on the omelette frittata and the cold Mango milkshake," I commented.

"I see. You want to work up an appetite first," he replied.

Then he gave me a knowing smile as he gazed at me. He flashed me some nice white teeth that made my pussy purr as I imagined his head dipping down between my widespread thighs and his lips sipping on my dangling labia.

I swallowed at my suddenly dry throat, turned to look away from him and stopped when I spied several packages laid out on the living room table. The largest package had pictures of actual sizes of butt plugs splashed across the front of it. The biggest one appeared to be twice the size of my two previous boyfriends' cocks. Would I be able to have something so huge thrust into my rear end?

Oh, boy. What have I gotten myself into?

Chapter Three

I jumped as Bill's apartment buzzer rang and he hurried to the speaker.

"Yup?" he answered.

"It's me," came Curtis' voice.

"Come on up," Bill spoke into the speaker and pressed a button on the wall.

"I thought you two guys lived together?" I asked. I'd heard they shared a woman in the past so I figured they lived together.

Bill gave me a surprised look.

"What made you think that?"

I didn't know how to answer that question, so I shrugged my shoulders.

Then his face conformed to one of understanding.

"Oh, you must have heard that Curtis and I shared a woman?"

My face heated and I nodded.

"We did. But we still keep our own places. She'd spend some nights here with me, or some nights with him at his place and sometimes the three of us together."

He seemed to be studying me. Was he curious for my reaction?

"That doesn't sound romantic. I mean, if you were sharing her, I would think she'd want to be with the two of you all the time?" I certainly would. But hey, I wasn't about to tell him that.

"She wanted it that way. We didn't. So we parted ways."

He was watching me again and suddenly things were feeling a bit confusing for me. This was supposed to be just a job assignment, I reminded myself and yet here I was mixing it up with my personal life. I really shouldn't be doing that. But I just couldn't help imagining living here with both men.

"Make yourself comfortable on the couch until Curtis gets here. He likes a beer when he comes over. Can I get you one? Or some red or white wine? Or something else?"

"White wine would be nice, thanks," I replied.

Geez. I'd had a couple of tequilas at the bar and now wine. They'd think I was an alcoholic if I weren't careful.

"You look really nice, Marty," Curtis complemented me several minutes later as the three of us sat on the living room sofa.

"Thanks." Too bad I had to dress up like a hooker to get compliments. And I just realized that Bill hadn't even praised me on my appearance when I'd first arrived.

How interesting and how rude. I'd dressed slutty in an ultra tight crimson red skirt, a matching red low V neck halter top which gave the men a very intimate look at the valley of my breasts and I wore matching red shoes with three-inch heels which made me look taller and gave my breasts an extra outward thrust.

I pushed aside my disappointment and was about to survey the items that Curtis had brought along and laid out beside the butt plugs and lube on the coffee table, when Bill suddenly clapped his hands, catching my attention.

His blue eyes flashed with excitement as he looked at me.

"Okay, let's get started. From here on out, Marty, you play the part of the hooker," Bill said.

I nodded.

"What do I need to do?" I asked.

"Number One rule. You do everything we ask. Without hesitation," Curtis answered. "Crazy Horse needs to see that we control your every move. He'll want a well-behaved woman. We won't be able to arrest him until he buys you. So we need to have you as submissive as possible in the hopes he'll bypass wanting to have sex with you before offering to buy you."

Hoping? This was the plan to keep Crazy Horse off me? Geez, it better work. Or I was screwed and I meant that quite literally.

"I can do that."

I just hoped I could get submissive. I had never been one to blindly follow a man. Maybe that's why I couldn't keep one? This assignment might be more challenging than I had anticipated.

"Let's get you outfitted with your first butt plug."

I nodded as anticipation raced through me.

"Where is the bathroom?" I asked.

As I reached out for the packages I would need, Bill's hand circled around my wrist, stopping me cold.

"What?" I snapped. I didn't like guys grabbing me without a reason.

"Second rule. You ask one of your pimps for permission before you do anything. And I mean anything. That includes going to the bathroom. Going to the bedroom. The kitchen. Masturbating. Anything."

I frowned. This was definitely harder than I thought it was going to be especially now that he'd gotten the word masturbating rolling around in my head. I would have to ask her permission to do that too?

Screw that shit. The minute I was back at my place, I was going to do just that.

"What are you thinking, Marty? I'm seeing defiance in your pretty blue eyes. We can't have defiance," Curtis said softly as he studied me.

Curtis didn't wait for an answer as he leaned forward and picked up the package with the plugs. As he gazed at me, his brown eyes looked kind of sleepy with what I could only perceive as to be a look of arousal. Beside him, Bill was opening the box containing the lube.

I swallowed with anticipation as sudden realization dawned on me. The *men* were going to insert the butt plug?

"Yes, Marty. No defiance. From here on out, any and all signs of boldness will be met with punishment. Is that understood?" Bill asked in a cool, demanding tone. His blue eyes penetrated through me and I could see he was quite serious.

"One little slip up, Marty, and Crazy Horse runs or kills us. We'll be going in unarmed ourselves and relying completely on the wire and backup," Curtis said as he withdrew a red butt plug from its box. Despite it being the smallest size, it looked quite big. I worried my lower lip as I wondered if that thing would fit inside me.

"These plugs are all sterilized, so no need to clean one before insertion for the first time. I want you to remove your clothes from your waist down."

Wow. The cool and casual way Curtis spoke had my entire lower half trembling with anticipation.

I blew out a tense breath as both men watched me.

"No hesitations, Marty. You are in this now or you are not," Bill prodded.

Shit. He was right.

Man, this was so incredibly difficult to be obedient. I nodded and stood.

Bill shook his head. Disappointment quite apparent in his gaze.

Frustration ripped through me.

"What?" I snapped.

"There were sentences said after my initial command. When this happens, you must ask permission in order to bring the topic back to where it should be."

"I see. My apologies, gentleman." I sat back down.

"Permission to stand and remove my clothing, sirs?" I forced myself not to say it through clenched teeth.

"I am detecting a little tension coming from Marty. Are you too, Curtis?"

Curtis stared at me. Butt plug in one hand and the lube bottle in the other hand. I was sure he was going to back me up and say, no, he didn't.

"I'm sensing the same. We will have to punish her later with the slave chains. You may proceed to remove your clothing, Marty."

I felt like cussing Curtis, but I held back. Slave chains? I wondered what that might be. Well, no use having more punishment doled out. Besides, they were right. I had to play hooker now. They were the bosses.

I forced myself to keep eye contact with Bill, who stood quite stiffly, his gaze locked to my hands as I slowly slipped my red miniskirt down over my hips. I let it drop, and it puddled at my feet. I trembled as both men fixated their gaze between my thighs.

My panties were black and quite sexy. The high leg briefs had strap detailing and a diamond shaped lacey area that covered my crotch and an area above the crack in my butt, fully exposing my curvy cheeks.

"Permission to remove my underwear, sirs," I asked and instantly realized my mistake. No sentences had been said after his initial command. It appeared that was acceptable as I wasn't reprimanded.

"Do it," Curtis answered in a hoarse voice. I could see the excitement flaring in his brown eyes. Noticed the tip of his pink tongue had appeared between his lips. Could feel awareness buzzing through me.

My hands trembled as I slid my fingers beneath the top black strap of the panty. I carefully watched the men as I lowered my underwear past my waist, over my wide hips and then I let the undergarment fall.

"Good girl," Bill praised.

"Now I want you to go to the end up the sofa. Hands on the arm rests, bend forward and legs spread wide," Curtis said. His voice sounded so cool and controlled that I wondered how often he said this to other women.

Jealousy zipped through me as I thought about the woman the two of them had shared. She must have been a complete idiot for not wanting two hot hunks in her bed every night.

"May I first remove my shoes?" I asked, remembering their earlier instruction.

"Yes, you may," Bill answered.

Both men watched as I bent over and undid the strap on one high heel and then the other. I'd angled my body in such a way as they got a pleasant view of my ass cheeks.

Suddenly I felt like such a tease, but I had to be careful. I needed to learn how to become a proper hooker and flaunting myself without their permission was a no no.

My face felt quite flushed as I slipped off my shoes, stepped out of my panties and skirt that had pooled at my ankles and then I held my breath as I moved to the end of the sofa, while both men watched.

Chapter Four

I felt both excited and nervous as I moved into position.

I was now bent over, my ass thrust out and both Curtis and Bill were quietly speaking to each other. Suddenly I felt ignored but I forced myself to be patient. They could be testing me.

I gazed sideways and realized none of the blinds had been pulled down on the windows. Was it possible that someone from another apartment building could see me? I *was* right in front of the window!

Should I bring this to their attention? Before I could come to a decision, both men stood.

Bill walked away, and I watched him open and then close the door behind him as he disappeared into another room, which I assumed was the bedroom.

Curtis slurped some lube onto the butt plug. He didn't look at me as he placed the lube onto the armrest beside my hand. Then he moved behind me and stood there.

I felt tense with anticipation and anxiety as I imagined his gaze roving along the contours of my backside. I almost jumped when he suddenly spoke.

"Bill and I were discussing that you should have a hooker name."

"Oh, really," I answered.

"We've decided on Blondie."

"Blondie is a nice name," I praised.

"From here on out, you'll be known as Blondie for your name. Answer to nothing else. We're undercover now, Blondie. Now let's get started with the insertion. By the time you're finished with these plugs, you will be open and ready for any man to take you."

Any man? I wondered why he'd used that choice of words.

I swallowed at my suddenly dry throat and wished for some gulps from the goblet of white wine I'd left sitting on the coffee table.

I could hear his breathing getting faster. And I inhaled as I felt his hot palms smooth over my ass cheeks. Then my cheeks were being pulled apart.

To my amazement, I could see Curtis' reflection in the window. One end of the butt plug, I was assuming the unlubed part, had been placed into his mouth like a baby's pacifier. He almost looked sexy hot with the plug between his lips.

I creamed hot as he picked up the tube of lube. I heard it squirt and felt the cool gel against my little hole.

I moaned as his finger pressed past the tight bundle of muscles and slid into me. I sucked in a breath at the foreign pressure as he slowly moved his digit deeper, pushing lube into me and against my anal muscles, which eagerly clenched around the intrusion

"You have a nicely shaped ass, Blondie. I can't wait to take it," Curtis said softly.

I trembled at his words and I wondered how he was able to talk with the plug in his mouth. I remained quiet as my attention was focused on what he was doing back there

Slowly, he withdrew. More slurps of lube followed. I felt a greater pressure as he inserted two fingers this time. He did the same thing as before, pushing in the lubricant and smoothing his fingers against my protesting muscles until they yielded to him.

"Okay, I think you're ready now, Blondie. Now what I want you to do is to breathe deeply, nice and slow and push gently as I insert. Understand?"

"Yes," I hissed.

"This is going to pinch. Maybe even hurt a little, but I want you to trust that I know what I am doing. Do you trust me, Blondie?"

"Yes." Gosh, I was sounding like a mindless submissive but I kind of liked this zombie feeling of letting him do all the work.

"Good. Now, we begin."

I could hear his breathing was getting louder and faster. So, was mine.

I involuntarily tensed my anal muscles as a smooth object pressed against my hole. Quickly, he slid the tapered end of the plug into me. My anal muscles clenched around it and I remembered that he had told me to push. So I did.

I could feel the thicker area of the plug now as it moved into me. The pressure had me moaning. There came some pinches of pain, and I grit my teeth, forcing myself not to swear or to squirm away. Then he was done and I breathed a sigh of relief.

However, my relief was short lived as the door where Bill had disappeared behind earlier, opened and Bill strolled out.

I gasped as I stared at him. He was completely nude.

He had a well-defined physique. Toned muscles everywhere. Broad shoulders, tight abdomen and he had quite a huge erection. I noticed he was wearing something black at the base of his cock.

A cock ring.

"You're going to have to start going poker face, Blondie. Crazy Horse doesn't want his hooker being too innocent in that she salivates when she sees a penis. You'll need to act professional like you see cocks every day. Like you'll do starting today."

Bill had come to stand in front of the sofa and I just couldn't take my gaze off his penis. It was abundant. Maybe three fingers thick and it was long. Very long. It was flushed an angry red and I assumed that was because the cock ring was doing its job in keeping him erect.

"Come and sit down on the sofa, in front of me," Bill instructed.

I gasped as the butt plug throbbed in my ass, as without hesitation, I moved my hands off the armchair and straightened. Then I went over and sat down.

"Good girl. You're improving with following your orders," he said with a smile.

I held back a grimace and stifled a retort of telling him to pat me on the head too, like I was a dog, while he was complimenting me.

"I am seeing a flare of defiance, Blondie," Bill chuckled.

Shoot! I merely smiled. I didn't want him to think I sucked at taking commands. I held my breath as he stepped in front of me. Not too close, but several feet away. This gave me an even closer look at his shaft.

It jerked as I stared.

"My cock likes you, Blondie. Take it into your mouth."

Holy smokes! Everything was suddenly getting very real.

A split second of telling him I was out of this assignment rushed through me, but my perfectionism of wanting a pristine work record and my curiosity about what was coming next, just wouldn't let me walk.

"By the fear in your eyes, you've never had a cock in your mouth? Am I correct in assuming this?"

"Yes," I answered meekly. Gosh, the man could read my inexperience like a book.

"By the time we're finished with you, tonight. You'll know everything you need to know on how to suck a man's cock. Now, remove your top."

My pussy clenched at his instruction.

I reached up and untied the ties. At the back of my neck. I dropped the straps and the halter fell away, allowing my breasts to pop free. Both men exhaled and I felt thrilled. They liked what they saw.

"Your breasts are exceptional. Like delicious hanging fruit, ripe for eating," Bill whispered.

Oh dear. The man had a way with words.

"I'm sure Crazy Horse will be impressed when he sees them," Curtis remarked. He was in the kitchen now, gazing into the fridge.

Huh, outfitting me with a plug must have worked up an appetite for him. Wish I could say the same. I was tense with anticipation and I should have felt complimented but the thought of being paraded nude in front of Crazy Horse was making me edgy.

I pushed away the nervousness and reminded myself that my sacrifices would help others. I decided not to thank them for their compliments. Instead, I waited for their next direction, which came pretty fast.

"Blondie, on your knees in front of me," Bill ordered. His voice sounded hoarse.

I hesitated, but remembered I was now undercover and learning the ropes.

Quickly, I dropped to my knees and gazed at the long, thick shaft right in front of me. My pussy quivered with want as I spied pre-cum glisten at the slit of his plum shaped cockhead.

"Wrap one hand around the base of my shaft," he said.

I trembled at his words as I envisioned his cock penetrating my pussy. I could feel warm wetness seeping from my vagina as I reached out and wrapped my right hand around his hot throbbing base.

"Now, as I insert my cock into your mouth, let it go to the back of your throat until it touches, then you pull your head back about an inch. Then wrap your other hand around my shaft so I can't thrust down your throat."

I did as he asked. I relished the powerful feel of his cock against my palms. Swallowed as I felt his flesh throb with wicked intent.

"Open your mouth. Never bite unless you are told to," he said in a warning tone.

Oh, sweet mercy. I couldn't believe I was actually doing this.

I parted my lips and he brought his hips forward until his cockhead sunk an inch between my lips. It felt weird having part of his penis in my mouth. But I kind of liked it. Liked that I had the power to pleasure him in this way. This was going to be interesting.

"Look up at me. I want you to watch my face at all times. Look for cues on my facial expressions. Do I like what you are doing? Do I seem I pleased? Am I in pain? Your mission is to please and to pleasure and that is all. You are the vessel for a man's pleasure. Nothing more. Is that clear?"

I nodded and gazed up at Bill and quaked at the sight of his blue eyes. They were dark and stormy. Aroused. Yeah, this is what I wanted to see. I wanted to see him pleased. Gosh, I must be insane to make this so personal.

Bill continued talking as he looked down at me with those heated eyes.

"Crazy Horse will request a demo before he decides if he wants to buy you or take you first before he decides to buy you. We could act like we're orgasming in front of him when you take me or Curtis into your mouth, but the real thing is best."

My head was spinning. Bill talked so casually, like he did this stuff every day. But then again, he was an undercover cop, maybe he did do these naughty things everyday?

One thing I was beginning to suspect. I might like doing this kind of undercover work in the future. It turned me on thinking I could get scum off the streets as well as explore my sexuality.

Yeah, it sounded mad. But I'd never been normal anyways, so why start now?

"Suck my cockhead. Nice and slow," Bill said.

Chapter Five

I tentatively hollowed out my cheeks and sucked. Bill gasped and I tried to read his facial expressions. His mouth was open and his eyes were closed. He looked happy.

I tightened my lips to increase the pressure.

He swore softly.

I caught movement from beside Bill. Curtis was standing there, observing. He was casually munching on a sandwich, seemingly enjoying what I was doing to Bill. In his other hand he held a glass of red wine.

I should have been embarrassed at having him watching, but I wasn't. I just wanted to impress and please. I moved my head forward, taking more of his rigid flesh into my mouth.

I wondered if maybe that was a no, no. Should I wait for instructions and just keep sucking? But I suddenly didn't care.

I gripped Bill's heated shaft tighter and moved my head so more of his cock was stuffed into my mouth. I began bobbing my head, bringing his shaft deeper in and then further out, before bringing him deeper in again.

I kept my gaze to his face, like he'd instructed. Back and forth, back and forth I went with my head. His velvet-encased shaft created such a delightful friction that my lips burned so wonderfully. His eyes remained closed and he was panting like crazy.

Suddenly, he reached out and grabbed the back of my head. I thought maybe he was going to stop me, but he just increased my bobbing by controlling the movement of my head. I didn't mind. I liked the power in his hands as he held me.

I just continued to slurp at his flesh. Licked my tongue against his shaft and used my teeth to give him a gentle sparkle of pain, all while I carefully watched his face for reactions. It appeared he loved everything I did to him. His face became flushed, his cheeks red. His chest heaved with every inhalation.

He was moaning too. His fingers slid through my hair and pain shrieked across my scalp as he gripped tightly. I winced but kept applying my new trade to his flexing flesh. His hold became more powerful and his pistoning strokes into my mouth, quite forceful. My slurps echoed through the air, mixing with his guttural groans. It was music to my ears. He really enjoyed the way I was pleasuring him. I was doing this right.

"I'm coming!" he suddenly ground between his gritted teeth. His thrusts grew quicker, deeper, stronger.

His cock was jerking in my mouth like a wild serpent. Then he was releasing.

I drank from him, swallowing every drop, knowing instinctively that's what he wanted. After I could suck no more from him, he withdrew.

"You may let go of me," he said in a hoarse voice.

I unclenched my hands and dropped them to my sides. Suddenly I hoped he would reach out and cup my breasts. I wanted his strong hands moving all over my body. Touching me. Pleasing me. Just like I'd pleased him.

My pussy was sopping wet and clenching and my anal muscles were throbbing around the intrusive plug.

Suddenly I just wanted cocks buried inside me.

"That was fantastic. You're a natural.," Bill hissed.

He stepped back and disappointment roared through me. But then hope flared as Curtis suddenly took Bill's place.

My breath halted in my lungs. Curtis was completely naked and he held several pairs of handcuffs in his hands.

"Follow me into the bedroom," he ordered.

Obediently, I followed Curtis into the bedroom. The room was huge, almost as big as the living room, kitchen, office combo. It had the same colour scheme in here as the rest of the apartment.

The walls were white and the furniture black. The floor was covered with a lush white wall-to-wall carpeting. I noted another door, closed, which must lead to an adjoining bathroom.

A black king-sized bed with four post canopy was set at a forty-five-degree angle near the corner of the bedroom. Pristine white sheer lace was held aside with decorative gold ties at each corner post and coffee-milk-colored comforters and chocolate brown-colored pillowcases adorned the bed. The comforters had been pulled aside, revealing black satin sheets.

Beyond the bed, there were floor to ceiling windows that lined the two walls. No blinds were pulled down on the windows, but I suddenly didn't care. Let people watch if they wanted.

The room was dimly lit with gorgeous gold wall sconces. Out the windows, I could see twilight had fallen and sparkling white stars burst in the grey blue sky. Buttery yellow lights twinkled in the faraway apartment windows.

"On the bed," Curtis coolly instructed.

Without thinking, I climbed onto the bed. The sheets were silky black and felt like soft velvet against my backside and legs as I sat down cross legged. I realized I had forgotten to breathe as I suddenly felt a tad lightheaded and overwhelmed with excitement and nervousness.

I inhaled slowly and tried to calm down. The air smelled richly of vanilla and I spied several flickering votives on the nearby bureau.

Curtis drew closer and my gaze flew to him. His mouth was hidden behind his shortly cropped beard and moustache, but his cheeks were flushed and his brown eyes were sparkling with excitement. The man appeared very fit and tanned. Muscles bulged all over his body and I could tell that he must pump weights. I dropped my gaze to the hair covered area between his thighs. His balls were swollen and his cock appeared very erect.

His cockhead was mushroom shaped, the stem quite red, engorged and jerked like a live electrical wire. His penis appeared just as thick as Bill's but several inches longer.

My ass clenched around the small butt plug as I imagined him sinking that juicy shaft into my behind.

My mouth was dry and my heart was beating fast as he studied me.

"You look scared and vulnerable," he whispered.

I felt flustered.

"I'm not...my experience is limited." I'd wanted to say I wasn't sure what to do next but remembered they would instruct me. I was supposed to be learning.

"We've gone over that already. So, don't be afraid. The vulnerable pouty look we need to keep. It makes you look so sexy. As to the lack of experience, we're giving you a crash course in that department. You'll be temporarily hooked on sex, so that's all you think about. Your eyes and body movements will show your need to Crazy Horse. We need to make you irresistible to him. Now lay down in the middle of the bed. This is your punishment for your earlier defiance. I've got four handcuffs. One each for your wrists and one each for your ankles."

My thoughts whirled. *Temporarily get me hooked on sex?* Who gets *temporarily* hooked on sex? My punishment? Gosh, I hoped they knew what they were doing.

Curtis moved to the head of the bed and I tensed at the gentle waterfall clinking of chains. From behind the left head poster he produced a long strand of chain. It was beautiful. Delicate and gold. The chain was very thin, like a bracelet thickness but so much longer and it sparkled like jewels in the dim lighting of the room.

"These are slave chains. One end attaches to the handcuff, the other end is clipped on an islet behind the poster. All four corners of the bed have one. You will be chained here, spread eagle, overnight while we take you. Any time you need the bathroom, one of us will take you there. If you have any objections as to what we are doing, you may leave now."

My thoughts whirled and my lower belly clenched at what he'd just said.

He was giving me an out, yet again. But he'd also said the words, *while we take you*. There wasn't an instant of those spoken words that made me want to leave.

"I'm in," I whispered as my pussy creamed with wetness.

Bring on the punishment!

Curtis nodded, looking quite pleased with himself.

I watched him as excitement rocked through me. I made sure I kept breathing to prevent light-headedness as he attached a handcuff to the chain, then laid the length of chain and cuff near my head like it was an offering. He did the same with the other three chains, bringing them out for me to see and then clipping the cuffs to the end of each strand and laying each strand out.

To my amazement, I didn't feel embarrassed being nude all splayed out for him. I was simply fascinated at his toned physique and that luscious plump shaft, which angled upward toward his belly and bounced with his every step. Sure, I'd seen a couple of guys naked before but they hadn't been well-hung as Curtis and Bill.

The mattress dipped as Curtis sat down near me. He reached out, lifted my left arm above my head and then snapped the chained cuff around my wrist. I realized the cuff was fur lined and quite comfortable.

He stood, then walked about, placing the other cuffs on my other limbs.

"Now you look spectacular. Like a slave goddess being offered to her gods," he said when he was finished.

I trembled at his words and blew out a slow breath as his hot gaze roved over my body. Appreciation sparkled in his eyes.

"Good, she's all prepared. Let the feasting begin," Bill's deep voice echoed throughout the bedroom.

My head snapped up to see him standing in the open doorway. A large, silver tray was perched in his hands. The tray was laden with several glasses of red wine.

Okay. This seemed a bit weird. I was restrained by my wrists and ankles and they were bringing in booze? What happened to them *taking* me all night?

Frustration zapped through me. I was aching to have sex done to me. I wanted to be at the mercy of their pleasure.

I frowned as Bill strolled into the bedroom with the tray.

"It's about time. I am so thirsty," Curtis complained.

He grabbed a glass of wine as Bill passed by him.

"Hey man, I'm not your servant, "Bill chuckled as he placed the tray on a nearby dresser and also grabbed a glass.

Both men fell silent. Leisurely, they sipped their wine and heat swished through my body as they viewed me. I could tell by their smiles that they liked what they saw.

Curtis' eyelids began to droop sexily as he continued to study my naked body. Bill's blue eyes flared hot as his gaze roved over my heaving breasts, my tummy and then ended at the juncture of my spread legs. My vagina clenched as I saw Bill's red tongue roll out and lick the droplets of wine from his lips.

I should say something to break the silence, but nothing came to mind. I just adored their perfect naked bodies, feeling hot and bothered, primed for action.

I jumped as Curtis suddenly sat down at the edge of the mattress and gazed over at me.

"Would you like some wine, Blondie?" he asked softly as his eyebrows lifted in question.

I nodded, wetting my dry lips with my tongue.

Curtis smiled. He placed his glass onto the night table, climbed onto the bed and moved closer until he was sitting near me. My gaze zeroed in on his shaft. It appeared quite erect, much more than moments earlier. Wicked heat continued to build through me at the sight.

Chapter Six

Then he reached over, grabbed his wine and drank. Droplets sparkled in his beard as he set his glass back down on the night table.

I frowned. Why would he offer me wine and then tease me like this?

Suddenly, his head was lowering and I felt the soft strands of his long hair tickle along my shoulder, my arm and then across my tender nipple and breast as his mouth melted over mine in an exploding kiss. His bristly beard and moustache chafed around the flesh surrounding my lips. Then I tasted the wine and quickly realized he was letting the liquid drip from his mouth slowly into my mouth.

Wow. This was different.

I relished the taste of man and wine as his lips delicately sipped at mine, dribbling wine into my mouth. I eagerly accepted and swallowed. He kissed me harder. I wanted more wine and I wanted *him*.

He pulled away, sipped more, placed the glass on the night table, returned to me and then his hot mouth melted over mine again. He dripped more sweetness and I swallowed like a baby bird. I swear wine never tasted so good.

He continued doing that for several more head-swooning kisses and I quickly became immersed in the pleasure; the hard feel of his lips crushing mine, the intoxicating raspy tickles of his facial hairs upon my flesh and the sultry softness of his long hair brushing my nipple and the curve of my breast.

I craved wrapping my arms around his neck to bring myself deeper into the kisses, but the restraints stopped me cold. I whimpered my frustration and he would simply draw me further into the succulent wine-drenched kisses, until I was moaning from the ultra-sensitive nerve endings that were sparking up needy fires all over my intimate parts.

Promptly Curtis pulled away. He was breathing harshly and I was panting.

"Do you like your wine?" he asked in a seductive tone.

"Yes," I breathed. I could see my breasts heaving from my deep breaths as I tried to calm myself.

"I knew you would. Bill and I picked spot on when we asked for you for this mission."

I blinked, confusion rocking me.

"But the Lieutenant said they were short-staffed and that's why I'd been given this assignment," I muttered.

The two men shook their heads.

Bill and Curtis had purposely picked me? Wow, how cool was that?

"We asked him to say that. We sensed you were sexually inexperienced and we didn't want you to think this was something romantic, especially since this is your first assignment of this kind," Curtis replied.

Ouch.

"Besides, newbies are easier to train," Bill added.

Double ouch!

"I don't think this is romance at all," I lied, feeling dejected and devastated.

Instantly I forced a blank poker face. I didn't want them to think I was some silly schoolgirl crushing on them and had just been rejected. Although I did feel that way.

Suddenly I just wanted to be gone. Swallowed up by the mattress. I mean, how embarrassing. Is this why they'd waited until I was bound and at their mercy before they told me the truth?

Boy, I'd been immature. Time to grow up and get on with my job. I was supposed to be a hooker. They wanted to hook me onto sex in order to carry out the assignment. So, be it.

Stupid idiot, am I? Okay, from here on out, this was going to be all business. I had to throw myself completely into my job. I gathered my courage and forced the harsh sting of rejection away.

I'd be the best hooker I could be and my work experience would shine when we caught Crazy Horse. I would soon be a detective, just like my brothers and my dad. Suddenly nothing else mattered.

Curtis studied me. Bill was doing the same as he stood near the dresser with the tray of wine-filled glasses. He was quiet and I tried to read his face but he was a blank.

I focused my attention back to Curtis, who was now nodding.

"Good. I am glad there are no illusions. It would just interfere with our work. Now let's get our pretty woman hooked on sex," Curtis growled.

His eyes twinkled mercilessly as he looked at Bill, who nodded. Bill lifted another glass of wine from the tray and I could hear the clinks of ice cubes hit the sides of the glass. He handed it to Curtis, who brought it over my left breast and tipped it.

I cried out as the icy liquid splashed on my nipple and dribbled all over my breast. Shivers raced through me and instantly my nipple tightened and grew cold.

It happened so fast; I didn't have a chance to anticipate what was happening until the icy contact.

I bit back a curse. I was in hooker mode now. I would have to endure or enjoy. I would choose the latter.

Suddenly Curtis' warm hand cupped my breast. His head dipped and then he sucked my cold, shocked nipple into his scorching hot mouth.

I pulled against the restraints, moaning as Curtis suckled. The motions of his mouth shocked fire into my hardened pebble. I could feel the solid length of his shaft pressing against my thigh as it burned my flesh with promise.

"Just feel, Blondie," Bill whispered.

He'd come to my other side and was holding a glass of red wine that tinkled with ice cubes. He sat upon the bed beside me and I tensed when he held out his glass, this time knowing what to expect.

I braced myself. My heart was thumping at an insane pace as Bill tipped the glass. Cold wine and tiny ice cubes splashed over my other nipple and trickled down the curves of my breast.

I cried out as Bill lowered his head. He cupped my breast and then took my nipple between his lips and started sucking as Curtis was doing.

My nipples felt hot and achy beneath the fiery tugs of their forceful mouths. My lower belly clenched, my ass gripped the plug and my vagina throbbed with heat and want. Then their tongues got into the action. Hot little whips lashed my nipples and their teeth were like sweet little daggers of pain as they nipped.

Eager lips pulled on my swollen cherry-colored nipples sending hot flashes of pulsing sensations deep into my pussy. The sexual torture of pleasure they created with those naughty mouths mingled with the pain.

Suddenly it was getting too intense. My nipples were turning into painful tips. Hard as rocks. My muscles were tightening all over my body. Heat was racing through me at lightning speed. My pussy was clenching with need.

Things were getting too intoxicating. Too hot. Too fast.

Again, I yanked at the chains, wanting to get away from their powerful mouths as they just kept sucking and slurping, tormenting my extremely sensitive nipples.

I was slowly losing my grip on sanity as I was literally being sucked toward a sea of sensual torment.

Oh boy, I was in big trouble.

Suddenly, their mouths left my throbbing nipples and then they were kissing the curves of my breasts. They were tender kisses and fiery kisses, followed by sharp teeth nipping, the pain quickly salved by hot tongues. The kisses and lapping and licking fired powerful sensations that were zipping like blades of luscious lightning bolts all over me and they were racing through me at an insane speed.

I kept my eyes closed, Just feeling.

Twisting. Falling. Dying for release.

One of the hot mouths moved off my breast, kissing scorching butterfly tingles across my belly. The other mouth remained at my breasts. Firm hands cupped me there, squishing my mounds together, giving easier access for kisses and nips to both my vulnerable nipples at the same time.

My body ached with need. My mind, fragmenting. Why had it been so easy for me to fall into this abyss of sensual torture?

I thrashed against the tinkling chains as the mattress dipped between my thighs.

Someone was dropping between my spread legs! Hot muscular shoulders pressed against my inner knees widening my legs even more.

I managed to open my heavy-lidded eyes and caught Curtis at my breasts. His eyes were closed and it appeared he was in some form of a zombie zone as his powerful lips kept sucking and kissing and lapping at my mounds. His hands massaged and kneaded my flesh until my breasts felt so swollen and ultra heavy. Until my nipples had grown to twice their size and were painful points like hard glass.

Puffs of warm air splashed against my engorged clitoris, making me lift my hips as I tried to get closer contact. Fingers pulled apart the soft lips of my labia to the point there was an exquisite stretching pain.

"I've never seen a woman cream so beautifully. Like luscious sparkling gems oozing out of you," Bill whispered. His voice sounded hoarse and his hot breaths scorched my pussy.

"Bill, please, take me. Fuck me," I begged. I needed penetration. My pussy was weeping so badly.

"Shhh, Blondie. You need to feel. Just feel. That's the only way we'll take down Crazy Horse," he answered.

Frustration snapped through me. Screw Crazy Horse. My muscles were getting sore. My body was too tight. My mind was freaking out. There were just too many fiery sensations popping up everywhere. I needed release.

I cried out to Curtis, begging for him to take me. But I was ignored. He just kept lapping and nibbling at my nipples.

Between my trembling thighs, Bill continued blowing air against my pussy, making my thighs clench against his shoulders. Making me moan as my pussy grew hotter and trembled with need. My quaking vagina continued to cream and it soon felt so heavy and swollen, just like my breasts.

I stilled as Bill let go of my labia.

A finger circled my clit like a vulture, creating sensations and quivers of need. I bucked and keened as my clitoris became engorged from the brutal pleasure. Powerful hands gripped my hips holding me still and then lips suddenly fused over my clit.

Bill sucked on my sensitive bundle of nerves and quickly built an inferno of pleasure. Swiftly I flew toward an orgasm. But then he backed off, leaving me panting and keening and struggling against his hands. Perspiration blossomed all over my body.

I just needed release!

I began begging again. Begging for someone to fuck me. Anyone! But they ignored me.

Sons of bitches!

Chapter Seven

B ill thrust his tongue into my vagina. My muscles clenched around the intrusion. But I couldn't climax. I knew his tongue wasn't big enough to give me any release. I needed a deeper penetration. He withdrew and thrust his tongue into me again. I could feel my juices seeping down my channel, heard him slurping as he sucked the cream out of me.

Oh, come on! He was drinking from me!

Tension continued to build.

They were torturing me. Making me needy. Making me nuts!

I thrashed against the restraints. Against Curtis' mouth as he suckled at my nipples. Against Bill's tight grip as he lapped and licked and penetrated my pussy with his tongue.

They were stoking an inferno deep inside of me. I could barely think now. I could only feel.

I was a throbbing pussy, an aching ass and two swollen breasts. I was a vehicle. An object for them to use. A body to endure pleasure and pain.

Suddenly I realized if they kept this up for a number of days, I *would* be hooked onto sex. Hell, I was already hooked.

"Easy, Blondie. Just keep still and you'll enjoy what's coming," Bill growled against my pussy.

I eagerly nodded. I believed him. I'd believe anything he said at this moment. I just needed satisfaction.

Curtis let go of a nipple with a pop and moved away. He stood at the bed beside me, stroking his shaft as he watched Bill rise over me. Bill's giant shaft was aiming straight for my pussy.

I creamed up a storm in anticipation.

"Please! Hurry!" I gasped.

I screamed and orgasmed the instant Bill's solid erection impaled me. Pleasure fire arced through me making me jerk against my restraints. Succulent spasms and fiery sensations rolled and wrapped around me and seared my insides.

The rest of his body came down upon me like a heavy blanket of heat. His mouth fused over mine and he swallowed my cries as I bucked against him. He maneuvered his hips and withdrew. Then he plunged his engorged cock into me again.

The intense fullness had me gasping into Bill's mouth as my pussy muscles clenched around him like a velvet glove. With his every thrust, he went deeper into me, stretching me and stroking the pleasure waves, driving them through me with a fury I had never experienced before.

He kept pistoning. Kept kissing me until I wasn't me anymore.

I was pleasure. I was pain. Lust and insane.

I was in hell. I was in heaven.

Man, I was confused.

My body twisted and jerked as searing convulsions engulfed me and he just kept thrusting. His hips moving rhythmically.

The pleasure came in tumultuous waves as his cock slammed into me, over and over. His lips were locked on my mouth, and he just kept catching my moans, my cries and my keening.

The orgasm was never ending. I was burning alive inside this pleasure. Even my brain was on fire. I was shuddering. I was experiencing a complete loss of control.

And I loved it.

Oh my God, It was *so* good. I wanted this to go on forever. Wanted to do this everyday. All day long. All night long.

All too soon my magnificent orgasm ebbed and Bill withdrew, climbing off me.

My head was spinning. My body was shaking. I had *never* experienced anything like this before.

Such intensity. Such depth.

I was panting, ready to doze off when I felt the mattress once again dip between my thighs. I could barely open my eyes as I peeked down to see what was happening.

Curtis had positioned himself between my spread legs. He was watching me, smiling mischievously, and he was tipping a glass of wine.

"It's far from over, Blondie. We're just getting started," he said with a smile.

Oh no! I cried out and jerked as the icy cold liquid splashed over my wonderfully aching pussy.

"Shh, Blondie. Just feel. All you need to do is feel. Don't think. Don't ever think," Curtis soothed. I tensed as his head dipped downward.

Suddenly Bill appeared at my left side. A glass of red wine held in his hand. He tilted the glass and splashed the icy contents over my pulsing nipple. He cupped my breast and then his head dipped downward.

"Just feel," Bill whispered, echoing Curtis' words.

And I did.

Scorching lips fused over my pussy and my nipple at the same time and I instantly flew into another orgasm.

You will be chained here, spread eagle, overnight while we take you.

The words that Curtis had said earlier while he'd been chaining me suddenly floated through my head as I jerked and convulsed within the pleasure waves. I suddenly realized I wasn't just sleeping over in chains after a session of hot sex. They meant they would fuck me all night. Over and over.

Wow, how had I not fully understood that?

And that's exactly what they did.

I don't know how I survived it. The pleasure they gave me drove me insane. Every time I awoke, one of them would take me. After each meal, they would take me. After showering, they would take me.

I needed the orgasms now, two weeks later, like a heroine addict needed a fix. I eagerly did what each man instructed me to do. Anything for my next climax. My next fix.

I didn't think. I just obeyed. I was mindless and I loved it.

They gave me orgasms that a woman should never experience. So beautiful. So addictive. So brilliantly mind shattering.

A couple of days ago, we'd had a photo shoot of my performance with Curtis and Bill. Pictures and videos would be circulated through the underground network informing pimps I was up for sale. We hoped Crazy Horse would want a meet. At this point, I didn't even care that Crazy Horse and his bodyguards would be there watching Bill and Curtis taking me. It would be just something exciting to experience in having strangers watching me climax.

Tonight, though, I was fidgety and anxious, just driving myself nuts thinking about what was going to happen next. Tonight, they would remove the largest butt plug that they had been inserted. I could hardly wait. My ass was so full, but I wanted something fuller.

How crazy was that?

The two men had used my pussy, nipples and breasts relentlessly, to the point all my intimate areas felt twice their size and I was so needy. Now I wanted my ass to be used too.

I'd been cooped up in Bill's apartment this whole time. The second day I'd been here, I'd learned one of the guys had already been to my apartment to gather my birth control pills and had made arrangements with a trusted neighbor of mine to water my plants and feed my two budgies, stating I'd been called home for a family emergency. These undercover cops sure did do their homework.

Bill and Curtis had both produced up-to-date medical clearances stating they didn't have any diseases, so condoms weren't used in order for me to get a better *feel*. A deeper addiction.

One man always stayed with me, so I wouldn't masturbate, which I was dying to do, while the other went out for food or to put the word out that Blondie was up for sale. So far, Crazy Horse hadn't taken the bait. But Curtis and Bill reassured me that undercover work took time.

I didn't have time. I wanted double penetration. And I wanted it now!

The apartment buzzer grabbed my attention. I got to the intercom first and I could hear Bill chuckling behind me as I asked who was there.

Exhilaration roared through me. It was Curtis. He had returned from the meeting to update the lieutenant.

I buzzed him in.

With Curtis returning it meant I would finally get my wish of double penetration with the two men.

I could hardly wait!

I was going to die from impatience.

Curtis was home, but the men wanted to have supper before our next sexfest could begin. Bill had volunteered to make his spicy Indian masala omelette frittata and a cold mango milkshake. The same thing he'd offered to me the first night I'd arrived here and yet tonight was the first time I'd have it.

It was only a little under two weeks ago that he'd offered to cook it, but it felt like a lifetime.

Back then it had irritated me to follow an instruction. Now I followed mindlessly. I was ready for Crazy Horse. I was just thinking that exact thought, while sitting on the sofa gazing out the living room window and inhaling the spicy scents of the omelets Bill was cooking when Curtis' cell phone rang.

Curtis, who'd been chatting with Bill in the kitchen, slid his device from his pocket.

Gosh, I couldn't get enough of looking at Curtis. He was just as sexy with his clothes on as without. His beard and moustache had been cleanly shaven and had stayed that way, because after the second day, I'd developed beard burn everywhere his mouth had been.

Who would have thought I'd be so sensitive to Curtis' hair?

I found myself grinning at him as he peered at the number on his cell and then took the call. While he talked on the phone he looked over at me. My smile fell as I gazed into his brown eyes. They didn't have the usual mischievous glint and he wasn't smiling. He was dead serious as he hung up the phone.

Bill must have noticed something was off too because he turned off the stove.

"What's up?" he asked.

"That was our contact. Crazy Horse wants to meet with us tomorrow night at a hotel he frequents. We're to bring Blondie," Curtis explained.

My mouth dropped open in shock.

Tomorrow night? Suddenly all my confidence was blown away.

"It's too soon," I whispered beneath my breath.

But the guys didn't hear me. I wanted to tell them that I didn't want our time together to finally be over. I wanted to stay here and have sex with them twenty-four seven.

Mentally I shook myself. I had to remember I was hooked. Soon I would have to get back to the real world. I just didn't know how I was going to wean myself off this awesome sex.

Bill nodded. His blue eyes flared with excitement.

"Blondie is ready. We'll introduce her to anal tonight. By the time we meet Crazy Horse, she'll know what to do. I've got the wires all prepared too. We just need to call backup in Vice and let them know where and when," Bill said.

"I'll call them later and set it all up," Curtis replied. He was still frowning and gazing at me.

Was he sad this was going to be over soon?

A sudden slap to Curtis' back from Bill had Curtis grimacing and then smiling again.

"Good stuff. Now come one, let's eat. Time to celebrate! You have permission to eat to your heart's content, Blondie. Come to the kitchen table," Bill said joyfully and he quickly headed back to the stove.

What was there to celebrate? I was going to lose my wonderful orgasms.

Chapter Eight

An hour later, I was lying face down on the bed, satiated from the delicious omelette and delightful milkshake.

And I was naked. My heart was racing with anticipation and I was gasping as Bill slowly pulled the large butt from me and then the delicious pressure was gone. When the plug was out, I felt lost and I almost wept from my ass feeling so open and empty. I craved for it to be filled again.

"Good job, Blondie," Bill said as he caressed my ass cheeks.

"Very good job. She's wide open and ready to be taken," Curtis replied in a hoarse voice as he peered at my behind.

A moment later the mattress dipped and I looked over to see Curtis lying down beside me.

He was naked. Stretched out. His hands leisurely tucked beneath his neck.

He appeared calm. But his erection was anything but calm. It was ultra-long and throbbingly thick, sticking straight up into the air like an angry flushed steel pole.

Heat blushed through me. My breathing quickened as I awaited his instructions.

"Climb onto me, Blondie. Impale your pussy on me. Ride me. But do not orgasm."

I trembled and nodded eagerly as I climbed over him. Then I squatted, inhaling as his thick hard cock slid deep inside me. Although he'd had me many times over the past two weeks, I'd never been ordered to ride him. This was an entirely new position and I found it intriguing. I also found the fullness of his thick, hot flesh stretching into me, exhilarating, to the point of breathtaking.

Within seconds I was riding him, grinding my tender clitoris against his shaft, and loving the tightness building through me.

"Permission to touch your chest?" I asked Curtis in the soft, submissive voice that the men had instructed me to always use during this assignment.

"Granted," he answered in a cool dominant voice.

He was studying me while I reached down and smoothed my hands over his warm hairy chest. I loved touching his chest. Enjoyed the rapid beat of his heart tapping against my fingers. It meant I was affecting him. His brown eyes were warm as he watched me and the ends of his red lips were upturned ever so gently. He seemed pleased with my obedience.

I put pressure on his chest with my hands and lifted my hips, bringing his ultra-thick cock out of me and then I sat down on him again, angling my body in such a way that my clitoris got perfectly massaged as I plunged his rigid length into me. I did it again and again, moaning softly with each impalement. In no time I got into a nice riding rhythm.

My breaths came faster. My lower tummy tightened and my inner thighs quivered. I was nearing the orgasm I'd been craving and I was thinking of defying his order not to climax, but his words reigned me in.

"Now I want you to stop," he ordered.

I moaned inwardly at my frustration. I did as I was told and sat still, leaving myself fully impaled on his throbbing shaft. The instinct to keep moving, to bring myself into climax was so strong that I almost defied him.

My breasts were heaving with my every breath and my pussy and ass were quivering with need. But I forced myself to be submissive. If

I failed the test tonight of not following orders, Bill and Curtis might cancel the meet tomorrow and despite myself being hooked on sex, I felt empathy for all the women I might be able to save from Crazy Horse.

Curtis lifted his hands from behind his head, reached out and cupped my breasts. His hot hands embraced me like I was a treasure. He gently massaged my flesh and I felt my vaginal muscles clench around his hot shaft.

"You have such beautiful breasts, Blondie. Crazy Horse is going to admire them. He's going to want to take you before he makes us an offer. I just know it," Curtis said.

I suddenly wished he wouldn't talk about work right now. I just wanted to be with the two of them.

I moaned as he tweaked my nipples with his thumb and forefinger. He rubbed my nubs until they were two rigid peaks of fire.

"Clamp her," Curtis instructed to Bill, who'd been silently watching. He was also naked and had been stroking his cock into one fine-looking erection. I trembled at just thinking of both of them pistoning their shafts into me.

Bill reached for something on a nearby dresser and then he strolled forward and outstretched his palm so I could see.

He held the most gorgeous nipple clamps. They looked like miniature crowns. They were gold and shimmered beneath the bedroom's pot lights. They also had what appeared to be a barbell that went right through the crown.

"These are magnetic clamps. They're similar to the ones you'll wear tomorrow night. The barbells are magnetic and pull apart so we can place the crown over the nipple, like this..."

He pulled apart each barbell and then placed the pretty metal crown over my nipple until it encircled my red rigid flesh nice and snug. Then he slid each barbell in until each one touched my nipple on each side.

"Voila. The clamps are adjustable for your comfort, so we can leave them on for as long as the clamps aren't cutting off blood supply. So if you can keep them on tomorrow night for as long as possible or near you, then backup can hear everything that is going on," Bill said.

I nodded as he placed the other gorgeous crown over my nipple and slid the bar bells into place.

I gazed down and loved my new princess look. The barbells coming out on each side of the crown gave my nipples a pierced look, which I found intriguing.

"These clamps don't have wires. But the ones tomorrow night will have a wire inside each of them, so our backup people can hear our conversations and be ready to come in. On the chance that Crazy Horse and his men want to take you into another room for some alone time, it will be up to you to get him to make an offer before he takes you, if that's possible," Bill said.

I nodded, not wanting to think about the strategy we'd worked out the last couple of weeks. I didn't want to think there was a good chance I might have to have sex with Crazy Horse and his bodyguards. Right now, all I could think about was getting my sex fix with my two vice department undercover cops.

Bill stood back and nodded.

"You look absolutely gorgeous, Princess Blondie," Bill praised.

"She's the best-looking hooker that Crazy Horse will ever see before he goes to jail," Curtis beamed up at me.

I smiled down at him, fully accepting his compliment.

"Now, Blondie, I want you to stay impaled on my shaft, bend forward and kiss me while Bill takes you from behind."

I just about came at Curtis' words.

Time for my double penetration!

Excitement flared and I moaned as I lay upon Curtis, my soft tummy meeting his hard masculine muscles and my breasts pressing against his chest with the nipple clamps digging beautifully into my flesh causing just the perfect blend of pain and pleasure.

I melted my lips over Curtis' mouth and then I shut off my brain and just felt the sensations begin to shimmer within me as we kissed.

Curtis' hands settled on my ass cheeks and I felt him pulling them apart. Awareness rocked me as I awaited Bill's next move.

Curtis deepened the kiss, thrusting his tongue into my mouth, sending spirals of arousal through me. Slurps of lube shot through the air and I kissed Curtis harder, trying to distract myself from what was about to happen.

I tensed as I felt something cool press against my open ass. It had to be Bill's finger. My sphincter eagerly clenched him as he entered and soothed lube against my anal muscles.

"She's nice and tight. Very responsive. I'll get a condom on after she's prepared" Bill said in a guttural tone.

Curtis moaned into my mouth. Perhaps he was answering Bill? I didn't care. Despite my increasing arousal, I felt tense with anticipation. A moment later, Bill pulled out his finger. More slurps of lube followed. Two digits slipped into my ass and spread the lubrication.

He withdrew.

His heavy breathing rippled through the air as I listened to him tearing plastic. It had to be the package containing the condom. I was fighting for breath now that Curtis' mouth possessed mine. He probably thought I was scared. I kind of was frightened. This was new to me.

More slurps of lube snapped through the air. I began to tense. What if it hurt? Bill was *so* big.

"Just relax, Blondie," came Bill's soothing voice.

I felt his strong hands upon my hips. He gripped me tight, as if he were afraid I might make a run for it. I inhaled as his lubed cockhead pushed against the entrance of my rear.

Oh, God.

Before I could so much as panic, the head of his cock entered me. I moaned as pressure split into me.

Oh yeah, Bill was definitely bigger than the last plug they'd just removed. So much bigger.

I ripped my mouth from Curtis and gasped for air as Bill withdrew.

"Easy, Blondie. I've got you, sweetie. There may be a bit of pain. But it won't hurt you bad. Do you trust me?" Bill asked.

I nodded and his hands tightened on my hips.

"Kiss me," Curtis growled. His brown eyes flared with eagerness.

I melted my lips over his mouth again as Bill's cock penetrated me. This time he impaled me so much deeper. Then he withdrew.

"Beautiful," he whispered. Despite my momentary panic, I was glad he was pleased.

Then he entered me again. This time he thrust so hard that he pushed Curtis' shaft against my tender clitoris, which sent arrays of pleasure whipping into me.

I moaned my approval.

Then he withdrew.

"No orgasming until Curtis and I come first. Understood?" Bill ordered.

Oh no! A hot slide of frustration grabbed me. But I nodded. I didn't even know how I could nod with Curtis' lips clamped so tightly against mine.

Bill thrust into me again.

Wicked sensations zipped over me and I could barely stop myself from gyrating my hips. Thankfully, Bill held me steadfast with his hands. The son of a bitch knew what he was doing, that's for sure.

He kept pistoning into my ass. Filling me to perfection. His cock stretched my anal muscles beautifully. With his every thrust, Curtis' penis jerked against my sensitive clit, firing it up with intense heat and making me desperate to extinguish the heated spasms threatening to burst within me.

When both cocks were inside me, I felt like I was bursting with pleasure. But when Bill withdrew, I felt sad and empty.

Soon his thrusts grew faster and faster. His cock grew thicker and slid deeper, making me shudder at the fierce penetrations. My abdominal muscles bunched into tight knots. My breathing grew so fast I felt like I was on a runaway freight train dashing into forbidden territory.

I keened as I struggled to hold back my orgasm. Moaned as Bill's pistoning went out of control.

Chapter Nine

S uddenly, Curtis ripped his mouth away.
"I'm coming!," he shouted.
"Me too!" Bill cried out.

His impalements grew fiercer.

I curled my hands into the comforters as I held back the orgasm that was building like an inferno. I just knew it was going to consume me, but I injected self-control. Just like I'd been ordered. It was torture, holding back my release. Absolute torment.

Perspiration blossomed all over my body as he kept pistoning. Beneath me, Curtis' body stiffened and then he was coming into me.

Jets of his sperm filled me, and then Bill quickly followed. His hot release spilled into me like a firestorm.

Bill's grip on my hips loosened and I gyrated like a mad woman in an uncontrollable dance between the two men's bodies as blades of pleasure exploded through me like a bomb.

I was mindless. In a frenzy as sizzling sensations overwhelmed me. I shuddered and convulsed as I rocked my hips, relishing the two cocks impaling me.

My mind was gone. My body was consumed by pleasure as I continued gyrating and embracing the spasms ripping through me.

It was so good. Too good. Beyond addictive.

I knew I'd want more in the future when this job was over. So much more. I knew I would never recover from this experience.

I was sexually hooked on these two men. Forever.

ALMOST TWENTY-FOUR hours had passed as Curtis, Bill and I strolled into the hotel lobby that the contact had indicated we were to meet Crazy Horse. I was dressed in a sexy dark chocolate colored mesh and leather outfit. The upper half was mesh with a daring collar and drooping open side sleeves, allowing Crazy Horse and pretty much everyone else in the lobby to see my crown-clamped breasts, as well as the delicate gold slave chains with black sapphire teardrops on each end, dangling from my clamped nipples.

My lower half was clad in a form fitting tight leather mini skirt. I wore no underwear. But I did wear some impressive matching brown leather high heel shoes.

I was nervous at something going wrong, but Bill and Curtis appeared smooth as silk as they flanked me on each side. The female at the front desk was watching us like a hawk as we neared her. Her smile was fake and I sensed she was already suspicious that we might be cops.

"May I help you?" she asked in a most business-like voice.

Her black hair was slicked back off her face. In the mirror behind her, I noticed she wore a fishnet over her severe bun. She was dressed in a stiffly pressed midnight blue uniform pant suit and the only makeup she wore was bright red lipstick. Her silver name plate stated her name as Anne.

I spied myself in the mirror and compared myself to her. I looked ravishing. After a hot shower, I'd dried, curled and brushed my long blonde tresses until they'd shone like gold. I'd used gold eyeshadow and black mascara which brought out the blue of my eyes. I'd followed up with a dusting of rose blush on my cheeks and nose and a pretty pink lipstick. I was dressed like a hooker, but I also looked smart.

The chocolate brown outfit had been the one I'd bought the day we'd been given the assignment and I'd saved it special for this night. I could still see Bill and Curtis' reaction when I'd stepped out of the bathroom wearing my attire. Their hot stares made me feel so powerful and their compliments of wanting to take me to bed right there and then had I not been wearing such a sexy dress had made me want to jump right into bed with the two of them.

I could see the front desk receptionist watching me. Her appreciative gaze was fixated to my breasts, the curves being quite prominent beneath the barely concealing mesh. I almost asked her if she wanted tips on how to dress nice, but I kept my mouth shut. It wasn't my business if she didn't want to look attractive to the incoming guests.

My gaze flew to Curtis and Bill. They looked so calm, but my heart felt like it was pounding out of my chest and my mind whirled with all kinds of scenarios of this meet going wrong. I gazed downward, trying to appear submissive, suddenly remembering that I should have been doing that from right from the instant we'd entered the hotel lobby, instead of peering curiously around at the luxurious crystal chandeliers and lush purple drapery on the ultra-tall narrow windows.

"Kurt and Bob with Blondie to see Crazy Horse. We have an appointment," Bill answered, giving her their fake names. To follow up, he popped a bubble from the gum he was chewing.

The woman tore her gaze from my breasts and her smile brightened. She nodded, said nothing and snapped her fingers.

From somewhere behind a nearby wall, a tall, burly bald man appeared. He was in his early thirties and I sensed this had to be one of Crazy Horse's bodyguards. He wore a shoulder holster with a gun and he had a nasty scowl as he motioned for us to follow him behind the wall from where he'd just appeared from.

The instant we were behind the wall, the bodyguard grabbed me by the waist and jammed the pistol right against my temple.

Shit. If my heart had been pounding before, it was going through the roof now. The guys had warned me to expect this but being in this position made me feel too powerless. The creep could have a shaky trigger finger and one wrong move from Curtis and Bill, it would be lights out for me.

"Drop all your weapons or I blow her head off," he said in a cool, calm voice.

Curtis and Bill raised their arms above their heads.

"Hey man, we were told to come unarmed. What are you? A cop? Hey, we don't know nothing. We'll just leave. No problem," Curtis said in a steel voice. I could tell he was pissed as he stared directly into my eyes, willing me to keep calm.

Another man suddenly appeared with a metal detector in hand. He was just as burly looking like the bald guy except with a full head of black hair and a mouth full of gold tapped teeth, which made me a bit nervous. He must like dentists.

He said nothing as he quickly waved the detector up and down both Bill and Curtis. No noise followed, which indicated no guns or knives.

Then he turned to me. His leery gaze zipped straight to my mesh top.

"Hi. Looking for a good time?" I whispered in my best hooker voice, feeling proud that my inner shakiness didn't show in my tone.

He barely nodded and I spied the tips of his lips upturn ever so slightly. Oh yeah, he was looking for a good time. I hoped it didn't have to come to that, especially because of those gold teeth that turned me off.

He waved his wand down my legs and then up my body and the metal detector alarm beeped mercilessly as it passed over my nipple clamp with the wire.

"Take off your top," the guy snarled as he let me go.

Shit! I was so screwed!

Like I wasn't wearing anything that wasn't already showing off my assets? Sheesh.

"Maybe we should go somewhere a bit more private," Bill broke in.

"Hey, Manuel, is that any way to talk to a lady?" Another man's guttural voice erupted from directly behind me. I twirled around and came face to face with the man who I recognized as Crazy Horse from the mug shots I'd been shown.

He was about a foot shorter than me. Heck, my heels didn't make me *that* tall.

He was staring directly into my eyes and I shivered at the evilness I spied lurking in those depths of shit brown-colored eyes. But I could see interest there too. Lots of interest.

Aside from being short, I knew he was Italian, had a bad temper, preferred blue-eyed blonde women and word on the streets had it that he had a leather fetish. Hence, my leather skirt.

"Sorry boss, but the alarm went off. I need to check out her nipple clamps."

"You'll do no such thing. That's my job. And what do you think? She's got a gun in those gorgeously crowned nipples?" he asked his minion as he continued to stare me down.

Finally I realized my mistake and cast my eyes downward and instinctively bit my bottom lip as I inwardly cursed myself.

Shit. I was screwing up big time. Forgetting things that I should not be forgetting.

"She appears to have a lot of spirit left in her. Apparently she's not fully broken yet," Crazy Horse stated as he began to walk around me.

"We thought it best left up to you. If you decide you want to buy her," Curtis replied.

"I'd like to mount her, is what I'd like. I have a room upstairs for a demonstration. Follow me."

I sighed inwardly. Too bad he hadn't taken the nibble Curtis had tossed out and acknowledged he was here to buy me. It would have been over, had he said that.

I just hoped our backup guys were paying attention in that discreet van nearby. Besides having a wire in one of the nipple clamps, there was also a tracking device in the other one. If they decided to take a *really* close look at the clamps, we were in trouble.

I could feel perspiration begin to blossom on my forehead as we followed Crazy Horse and his two bodyguards onto the elevator. It was hot in here and the fluorescent lights made everything too bright. Not to mention all the walls having mirrors which sent reflections of light all around us.

The elevator began to ascend.

"I hope you have a room with a relaxing view. Blondie likes looking out the windows when she's taken by two men," Bill said coolly.

"I noticed that in the video and pictures you circulated," Crazy Horse said.

My thoughts returned to the photo shoot I'd had with Bill and Curtis having sex with me in the living room on the sofa. That had been one hot session, but that had been before my introduction into double penetration. Just thinking about having them double penetrate me again had me wanting it. I nervously sucked on my lower lip and noticed Crazy Horse was watching me again.

Oh boy.

Suddenly Crazy Horse reached out and pressed a red button on the console. The elevator came to an abrupt stop.

Oh. Oh. Not good.

He turned to Bill and Curtis and smiled.

"I want you two to take her right here in the elevator, with us watching."

Chapter Ten

I closed my eyes as my stomach sank. I'd been warned this request would most likely happen. It was a way for Crazy Horse to assure himself we weren't cops. He probably figured cops wouldn't have sex in front of him and if he said something wrong in the elevator, he'd have time to make it to another floor to escape before backup arrived.

Boy was he ever wrong. I was anxious for sex.

Now I understood why I'd been hooked on it. Just having Bill and Curtis nearby had my body humming. And having complete strangers watching...didn't turn me off in the least bit. I turned my mind toward the numerous women that would be saved if I went through with this and caught this man.

It would be worth it.

I was pretty tense as I awaited an instruction from Bill or Curtis.

"Listen, man. She's a Queen. Screwing her in an elevator is so uncool. If you have the slightest interest in buying her, then we don't want her demeaned in an elevator. Have some class, man. We would appreciate a nice cozy room with a comfortable bed for her and us. And for you so you and your people can taste the merchandise before you decide if you will buy her or not. Or we're just going to have to take our business elsewhere. If you don't buy her, we have another pimp who has expressed interest and that's where we're heading afterwards or sooner if you can't accommodate the lady properly. I doubt our other interested party will be playing such games with us. Understood?" Curtis said in a controlling do-not-argue-with-me voice.

A muscle twitched in Crazy Horse's cheek. He said nothing for a moment as he studied me in the mirror. I demurely raised my gaze, gave him a submissive smile and then lowered my eyes again.

He swore softly. I noticed a very bold erection pressing against his pants. I trembled as my body reacted.

"She wants me. I can tell," Crazy Horse said.

"Boss...watch your words," one of the bodyguards murmured.

"Shut the fuck up!" he snapped.

Okay, Crazy Horse was definitely excited. I do believe I had him hooked. Another thing I remembered about him was when he got enthusiastic, he became focused intently on what he wanted and he didn't think straight. In other words, he was impulsive.

Suddenly I went beyond everything I'd been taught over the past two weeks of being submissive and not doing anything unless I was told to, and boldly reached out and slipped my fingers against his cool, sweaty palm. I kept my gaze down and bit my lower lip pretending I was like a shy little girl. I swallowed tightly as he gently squeezed my fingers.

"Okay, let's go up to the room. But I don't want anyone touching her but me. She's mine now," Crazy Horse said in a high-pitched voice.

Curtis nodded. He reached out and pushed the button to go up.

"Just remember you only get her if the price is right and you don't damage the goods while taking her for a ride. I need her in tiptop shape for the other possible sale. You understand how these things go," Curtis said.

"We'll discuss the price for her, after I take her," Crazy Horse replied.

My heart pounded insanely as a minute later, the elevator door slid open.

Crazy Horse had the stupidest happy grin on his face as he yanked me out into the hallway with him like he already owned me. His two bodyguards flanked him, their pistols drawn as if waiting for trouble. Bill and Curtis came up the rear.

My heart was pounding even harder as we stopped in front of room 666. It appeared what had been said in the elevator wasn't good enough to take down Crazy Horse as no jackets had shown up. That meant I would have to entertain him.

Now that the time had come, I wasn't sure I could even go through with it.

Suddenly there were shouts all around as people in uniform swarmed us.

"Freeze! Vice Squad! Everyone! Put your hands up!"

TWELVE HOURS HAD PASSED since Crazy Horse and his two bodyguards' arrest.

Bill, Curtis and I had given our statements and I was getting so many appreciative looks from my fellow male officers that Curtis insisted I wear his brown leather jacket so the men couldn't see my breasts. He even zipped the coat up nice and tight beneath my neck. I swear if there had been a lock on the zipper, he would have locked that too.

Bill always had a scowl on his face as he shot dagger gazes at the cops who ogled me and I found it amusing. I began to wonder if Bill and Curtis might be jealous?

That last thought thrilled me as the three of us rode quietly in the elevator up to Bill's apartment. Bill had asked me to accompany him home and get my stuff, and Curtis had come along to get his things as well.

I was trembling too, from sex withdrawal as this was the longest I had gone without sex since this whole assignment had started. I was also feeling irritable and tired. I just wanted to go home, do some heavy duty masturbating in order to take the edge off, if I could, and sleep for the four days that the Lieutenant had given us off. But it appeared Curtis and Bill had other plans for me.

The instant we were all inside Bill's apartment and the door closed behind me, the two men were quickly assisting me in removing Curtis' leather jacket. But when their hands flew to my waist, one set ready to lift my top and the other pair of hands about to drop my skirt, I slapped their hands away and stopped them cold with a harsh *no*.

That single word made them freeze and by their shocked looks, you'd think I'd just dumped a bucket of ice water over their heads.

"Listen, guys. I'm not a hooker anymore. My name is Marty, not Blondie. And I'll say when you can fuck me from here on out. But if you want me, I have conditions."

Both men's eyes narrowed with suspicion.

I continued as I stared at Curtis. My heart was thumping a mile a minute at what I was about to say.

"Here's the thing. At the beginning of this assignment I was told that I was just an assignment and I should not read anything more into it."

Curtis frowned. "Yeah, I had to say that because I wanted you to focus on the work and not on us."

I was grateful to hear that. I truly was. That meant there was hope for a relationship.

"It didn't work for long because over the past two weeks I was sensing you two were enjoying the sex a bit too much."

"Is there any other way to enjoy it?" Bill asked with a chuckle.

Beside him, Curtis nodded.

I smiled inwardly as I focused on the two men.

"Here's the thing. You've got two choices. Number one. You let me get my things and let me be on my way so I can masturbate my way out of this addiction that you two have screwed into me. Or..."

I paused for effect until I could see I had their undivided attention.

One pair of blue eyes and one pair of brown eyes stared back at me with an eagerness in their gazes that had me almost forgetting about my conditions and just asking them to take me right here and now.

I blew out a tense breath and tried to calm myself.

"Choice number two. The three of us move in together so I have access to you, whenever I need my fix until I deem myself cured of this affliction."

"And if you're never cured?" Curtis asked softly.

"Then you're stuck with me. So? What will it be? Number one or number two?"

I usually wasn't such a bold person, but the past two weeks of having to be submissive taught me that I would rather keep my power and demand what I wanted and needed instead of daydreaming about it and giving my power to someone else in the hopes they might make my dreams come true. If I picked the latter, my dreams may never come true and I just know I'd have tons of regrets not doing what I wanted to do from here on out. And I wanted them.

Curtis and Bill remained silent. Their faces had turned cool and calm, just like they'd been while I'd almost been man handled by Crazy Horse's bodyguards.

Shoot. Was I being too aggressive? Maybe they had decided I wasn't for them?

"An answer would be nice," I snapped as my irritation grabbed hold.

"We were in the process of giving you our answer when we first walked in," Bill replied with a smile. "Tearing off my clothes?" I asked.

Curtis stepped forward, took my hands into his and squeezed gently.

"Hey, baby. If you prefer we go nice and slow." He let the sentence dangle.

I blew out another tense breath. I wanted to stomp my feet in frustration. Why weren't they giving me a proper answer?

"Nice and slow and then send me on my way? Or nice and slow, the three of us are moving in together?"

Curtis gently pulled me down the hallway and into the living room, where I stopped cold.

Set in front of one of the windows on the shady area of the living room I spied my two yellow budgies in their cage, as well as the several plants I'd had in my apartment, which had been set in the sunshine on the floor. It appeared that one of the guys had snuck out of the precinct after giving a statement and gone to my apartment to bring my birds and plants here.

Happiness rocked me. I had my answer.

"How did you know this is what I wanted?" I asked, as emotions, thick and raw bubbled up from my chest.

I was so happy to see my birds appeared well and all my plants were thriving.

"Well, the steamy way you've always looked at us, even before the assignment. It wasn't hard to figure out that you wanted us. Not to mention you seemed to enjoy the sex a little bit too much over the past two weeks," Bill answered with a grin.

"Now, may we undress you, our queen?" Curtis asked.

I trembled as both men studied me, awaiting my reaction.

"Only if you supply me with more crown nipple clamps. Vice took mine as evidence," I replied with a pout.

"Your wish is our command. Follow us into the bathroom, our queen. We deem it necessary to give you a nice hot shower."

I was delirious with happiness when not too long after, my nipples were once again crown clamped. The pressure and touch of pain were exquisite as they throbbed. Now I stood sandwiched between Curtis and Bill, the steamy hot shower spray drenching the three of us.

They had wasted no time. My pussy muscles gripped Bill's shaft every time he entered my quaking wet vagina and my anal muscles spasmed around Curtis' cock as he entered and then left me.

The two men had quickly gotten into a driving rhythm that had me gasping for air and jerking between their hot bodies as pulsing sensations spun through me. Their hot palms smoothed over my curves, soaping my flesh with delicious massages and soon my tummy tightened and my inner thighs trembled.

Then without warning, I exploded.

An orgasm tore through me like a tornado. I was filled with cocks and pounded by pleasure. It was mind bending at how both men continued to piston into me while I convulsed between them.

One in. One out.

Their continued pistons allowed me to enjoy the wrenching spasms me until I could hardly stand anymore.

When I came down from one climax, they quickly fucked me into another one.

This was perfect. I just know that living here with these two cops was going to be everything I had ever dreamed it might be.

Yes. I was living my dream of being taken by two cops. And I loved it!

The End

Spunky Girl Publishing Catalog

Jasmine Black
~Erotica~Without the
Romance

Here are some more Jasmine Black eBooks...

Taken by Two Cowboys

———— ∝⦿∞ ————

Sierra Allan works hard at her late-father's horse ranch. When her
step-brother adds her handy girl services to a private auction to help
raise money for the failing ranch, she figures there's no harm...but she's

stunned when her services are sold to two sexy cowboys who give her an erotic way to save the ranch—submitting to their dark desires..

Taken by Three Billionaires

Billionaire friends, Liam, Theo and Elijah have just won Princess Isabella in a billionaire card game. Isabella knows exactly what the three men will want from her...she just hadn't expected to have all three of them at once!

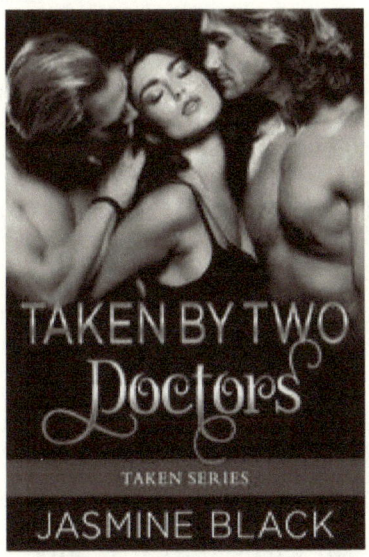

Taken by Two Doctors
A BDSM Medical Fetish Erotica Quickie MFM

Waitress Jean Spelling visits her controversial doctor once a month for some much-needed...stress relief. She looks forward to putting her feet up in the stirrups and enjoys Dr. Ball's naughty unconventional treatments. This time when she arrives, she's surprised to discover that she'll be physically examined by two doctors and they'll prescribe her some much-needed release right there on the examination table!

Stories in Jasmine Black's Ménage series

Stories in Jasmine Black's Taken series

Jasmine Black Website ~ http://www.jasmine-black.com
Twitter ~ @blackerotica1

Jan Springer ~ Erotic Romance

Cowboys For Christmas
Cowboys Online 1 ~ Moose Ranch
Jan Springer
A Canadian Contemporary Ménage Romance m/f/m/m Series

Jennifer Jane (JJ) Watson has spent the past ten Christmases in a maximum-security prison.

The last thing she expects is to get early parole, along with a job on a remote Canadian cattle ranch serving Christmas holiday dinners to three of the sexiest cowboys she's ever met!

Rafe, Brady and Dan thought they were getting a couple of male ex-cons to help out around their secluded ranch, but instead they get an attractive and very appealing female.

In the snowbound wilds of Northern Ontario, female companionship is rare.

It's a good thing the three men like to share...

They're dominating, sexy-as-sin and they fill JJ with the hottest ménage fantasies she's ever had. Suddenly she's craving cowboys for Christmas and wishing for something she knows she can never have...a happily ever after.

Cowboys In Her Pocket
Cowboys Online 2 ~ Moose Ranch
Jan Springer

*After spending ten years in a maximum-security prison Jennifer Jane (JJ)
Watson got early parole and a job on a remote Canadian cattle ranch
playing housekeeper to three of the sexiest cowboys she's ever met...*

Spring has finally arrived at Moose Ranch, and a single woman fresh
out of prison shouldn't be experiencing scorching ménages with her
three sexy-as-sin cowboys. But JJ's love for her men continues to grow
as she gives into the fevered heat and scorching passions she feels for
each of them.

Life is perfect.

Until her new life is tested when mysterious happenings occur on the
ranch and then one of her cowboys is viciously attacked and injured.

Will JJ's newfound freedom and happiness be ripped away?

Rafe, Brady and Dan never expected to find an attractive and very appealing female to help them out at their secluded ranch. But in the wilds of Northern Ontario, female companionship is rare. It's a good thing the three men like to share...

Brady, Dan and Rafe have never been happier. Their cattle ranch is flourishing and their continued desire to share the sexy woman who cares for them makes their life complete. Until danger threatens to rip everything apart...

Loving Her Cowboys
Cowboys Online 3 ~ Moose Ranch
Jan Springer

AFTER SPENDING TEN years in a maximum-security prison Jennifer Jane (JJ) Watson got early parole and a job on a remote Canadian cattle ranch playing housekeeper to three of the sexiest cowboys she's ever met...

Her love for her cowboys continues to grow as she gives into fevered heat. But JJ's simmering restlessness explodes and she's seriously making up for lost time by pursuing her dreams. There's only one little problem. She hasn't revealed to her bosses what she's been up to while they're away tending to the cattle. She knows when they discover her secret, there will be hell to pay.

Ranchers Rafe, Dan and Brady have found the woman who completes them. She makes their secluded ranch a home-sweet-home. She's vulnerable, sweet and willing to share her bed with all three of them. But when JJ's secret is unwittingly revealed, they're stunned and angry. They figure it's time to dole out some fiery punishment in some mighty naughty ways...

Cowboys In Her Heart
Cowboys Online #4

AFTER SPENDING TEN years in a maximum-security prison, JJ gets unexpected parole and a job on a Canadian ranch serving up scrumptious dinners and lots of hot love to three of the sexiest cowboys she's ever met.

Jennifer Jane "JJ" Watson has never been happier. She's going to have a baby!

Thankfully, their wilderness ranch is a nice distraction for her three sexy cowboys while she's away flying her plane. But when she's home, her dominant hunks are tending to her naughty pregnant cravings and that includes plenty of sizzling ménages.

Rafe, Brady and Dan don't much like the idea of their woman flying the Canadian skies and being at the mercy of the unpredictable Northern Ontario weather. They would prefer having her warming their beds twenty-four seven. But she has a way of getting what she wants and right now she needs her new-found freedom.

Worst fears are realized when JJ, her friend and JJ's plane suddenly go missing and she doesn't come back home to them.

Always Her Cowboys
Cowboys Online 5 ~ Moose Ranch

Reader Advisory: Best to read in order. 1. Cowboys for Christmas, 2. Cowboys in Her Pocket, 3. Loving Her Cowboys, 4.Cowboys in Her Heart, 5. Always Her Cowboys. 6. Her Forever Cowboys 7. Claiming Her Cowboys

A Canadian Contemporary Ménage Romance m/f/m/m

JENNIFER JANE (JJ) Watson has spent ten Christmases in a maximum-security prison. The last thing she expected was to get early parole, along with a job on a remote Canadian cattle ranch serving Christmas holiday dinners to three of the sexiest cowboys she's ever met!

Rafe, Brady and Dan thought they were getting male ex-cons to help out around their secluded ranch, but instead they got an attractive and very appealing female. In the snowbound wilds of Northern Ontario, female companionship is rare. It's a good thing the three men like to share...

Christmas is coming once again to Moose Ranch and with JJ's due date approaching, she's distracting herself from anxiety attacks by

1. https://janspringerauthor.files.wordpress.com/2017/11/alwayshercowboys_ebook-1new.jpg

keeping herself ultra-busy preparing for the arrival of her baby and planning Moose Ranch's first annual Christmas party!

In having a wee baby on the way, there's a lot of stress for Brady, Rafe and Dan. Especially due to JJ's decision on having a wilderness mid-wife deliver the baby *at their secluded ranch* - with *all* of them present for the birth! But their concerns don't stop the men from showing JJ how much they love her...out of bed and in!

With wicked snowstorms, a grounded bush plane, a cheerful holiday party and a sweet baby on the way, the owners of Moose Ranch know this will be one sparkling Christmas season they won't soon forget...

PLUS: HER FOREVER COWBOYS ~ Snowy Creek Ranch #1 Cowboys Online #6

Claiming Her Cowboys ~ Moose Ranch #6 Cowboys Online #7

Risqué Girl Delights Boxed Set
(Contemporary Erotic Romance)

...a touch of romance, a ménage or both?

Edible Delights

YEARS AGO ALLIE MASTERS lost herself in the scorching passion of a ménage a trois relationship with her two bosses. In order to regain her independence, she walked away.

Max and Nick were very fulfilled with their gorgeous assistant. The lovemaking was breathtaking and both men willingly shared the woman they wanted to spend the rest of their lives with. Then she left.

Now Max and Nick have decided it's time to seduce Allie back into their lives.

Toygasm

IT'S A CASE OF MISTAKEN identity when the two owners of Sexy Toys, show up for an erotic several day photo shoot of their toys with famous nude model Cammie Creek.

---

2. https://janspringerauthor.files.wordpress.com/2015/02/rgdelights_box_js_3d_noshadow-1.jpg

Cammie believes the two hunks are the male models she's supposed to work with. Usually she doesn't mix business with pleasure, but when they're seducing her right there in front of the camera, she can't resist turning them into her own personal naughty toys.

Josh and Jode are enjoying the perks of being male models; hot lust, sizzling toys and the best pleasure they've ever had. But how will Cammie react when she discovers they're actually her bosses and not just male models?

Shy Girl

FINALLY FREE OF AN abusive relationship, "Shy Girl" Emma McCall sheds her inhibitions and explores her sensual side at Club Rendezvous, a club specializing in the Alternate Lifestyle.

At the club she's surprised to find Logan Masters, a sexy hunk she's secretly fantasized about since college. With Logan's help, Emma will experience her ultimate fantasy - a scorching ménage a trois.

Roman and Julietta

HER PERFECT LOVER...

Modern day pirate Julietta Black's life has always been immersed in the violent and traditional ways of piracy. When her family's arch enemy puts a hit out on her family, Julietta knows there's only one way to lift the hit; she must kidnap the enemy's sexy grandson and force a union between the two warring families. Night after night, wrapped in Roman's strong arms, she can't deny the searing attraction blazing between them. Nor can she deny he now holds her heart as well as her life in his hands.

His dream angel...

When Roman Prince's mysterious captor offers him a luscious woman to bed, fierce desire ignites, melting his usually tight self-control. Lust quickly turns to love as he enjoys their naughty trysts more than he should. How will he react when he discovers he's been kidnapped, not for a ransom, but captured for his sperm?

Alpha Outlaws Boxed Set (Books 1-5 Outlaw Lovers)
5 Books!!

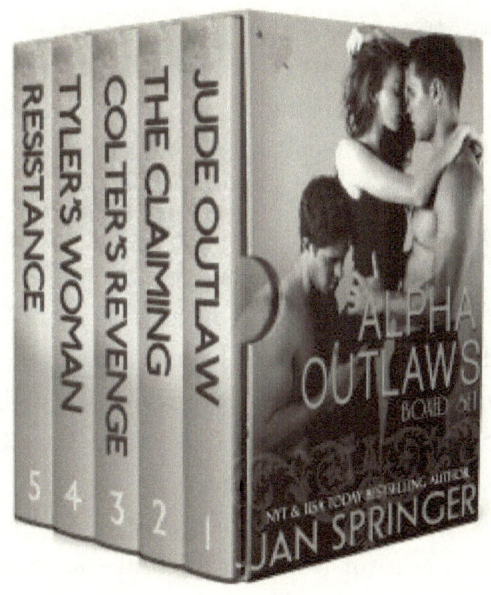

3

IN A WORLD GONE MAD...

A fast-acting virus has killed a majority of the world's female population. With the creation of The Claiming Law, groups of men suddenly have the right to claim a female as their sensual property and the sexy Outlaw brothers are going to declare ownership of the women they love...any way they can.

Jude Outlaw

When Cate Callahan learns Jude is coming home from the Terrorist Wars and is ready to claim her under the new law—with the help of his four brothers—she steals their boat and escapes to the high seas. Unfortunately, her runaway bid for freedom doesn't last long.

Quickly capturing his lover, Jude rekindles the flames and seduces Cate back into his bed.

---

3. https://janspringerauthor.files.wordpress.com/2010/07/alphaoutlaws_js_box_final.jpg

But Jude holds a secret that could make him lose Cate forever...
PLUS

The Claiming

Seeking refuge from the Claiming Law, Callie Callahan hides in a deserted cabin in the Maine woods and is shocked when her ex-flame finds her. She's always craved being in Luke Outlaw's arms. Tasting him. Touching him. Taking him deeply within her. So, what's a girl to do but to delve into the sinful delights he offers.

Luke has finally reunited with the love of his life. He knows there is only one way to keep Callie safe and with him forever. He'll do it with the help of his three brothers and an assortment of naughty toys. Rekindling the flames between them, he unleashes Callie's sensual side, taking her in ways she never dreamed possible, all with the ultimate goal of introducing her to the Outlaw Lovers and The Claiming.

Colter's Revenge

Revenge belongs to Dr. Colter Outlaw when he unexpectedly reunites with the beautiful woman who broke his heart during the Terrorist Wars. Capturing her, collaring her and holding her against her will, he seduces her, fills her with wicked desires and naughty cravings for a delicious ménage. Fully intent on breaking her heart and walking away, Colter's plans unravel when he submits to the carnal pleasures Ashley gives him so freely.

Colter had told her he loved her. He'd whispered promises of rescue from her life as a slave, but when he'd suddenly disappeared, she'd been devastated. Infected with a version of the X-virus that leaves Ashley Blakely sexually excited on a daily basis, she has come to Pleasure Palace to bid on a cure for her illness. She never expected her Outlaw Lover to be there and screw her plans. Nor did she expect to give him her heart and body so easily...

Tyler's Woman

For years Tyler Outlaw and his best friend, Hunter Brown, endured brutal torture and worse in an overseas terrorist prison. Finally, free of their hell, they return home intent on seducing Laurie into their erotic-filled fantasies.

Laurie Callahan has always experienced red-hot pleasure and passionate love in Tyler Outlaw's arms. But when he's pronounced MIA, presumed dead in the Terrorist Wars, Laurie's world is shattered, and her heart is broken.

Shocked to discover Tyler is alive and he's taken a male lover, Laurie is thrust into a sensual world of sizzling seductions, scorching ménages and the carnal desires that both scarred men crave. But she fears Tyler won't want her when he discovers she's not the same woman he left behind...

****READER CAUTION IS ADVISED (m/m forced scenes) ****

Resistance

In the near future, a virus has been unleashed, killing a majority of the world's female population, forcing the introduction of the Claiming Law. A law that states men have all the rights and women are sexual property claimable by groups of men.

Fugitive female...

Renegade Resistance leader Reena "Red" Wilde is in for the fight of her life when she experiences an erotic attraction to the two most dangerous men she's ever met.

Black ops assassin...

Months ago, Will "Blade" Smith spent one sizzling evening in the arms of a red-haired seductress. Now she's his next assignment. One look into her gorgeous eyes and he's wrestling his heated cravings for her all over again.

Bounty Hunter...

When Cade Outlaw nabs his bounty, sexy-as-sin Reena Wilde, his profession dictates she's hands-off. But he can't ignore the magnetic sparks between them...or that she is the biggest temptation of his life.

Resistance is futile...

After Reena escapes Cade and Will and falls prey to a band of evil hunters, she's grateful her sexy hunks come to her rescue...and in return, saves their lives. Trapped in a solitary cabin during a wicked snowstorm, she can't resist her two, well-hung studs, nor can she deny they've claimed her heart.

Many more Jasmine Black and Jan Springer eBooks, print books, audiobooks plus translated eBooks and print books can be found at http://www.janspringer.com and http://www.jasmine-black.com

Here are ways we can connect:

Jasmine Black Website at http://janspringerauthor.wordpress.com/jasmine-black/

Jan Springer Website at http://www.janspringer.com[1]

Instagram – http://www.instagram.com/janspringerauthor

Facebook - https://www.facebook.com/janspringereroticromance

Twitter Jan Springer- https://twitter.com/janspringer @janspringer

Twitter Jasmine Black - https://twitter.com/blackerotica1 @blackerotica1

Pinterest - http://www.pinterest.com/janspringer1/

Jan's Blog - http://janspringerauthor.wordpress.com/blog-2/

Happy Reading,

Jasmine Black / Jan Springer

---

1.   http://www.janspringer.com/

Don't miss out!

Visit the website below and you can sign up to receive emails whenever Jasmine Black publishes a new book. There's no charge and no obligation.

https://books2read.com/r/B-A-GIJD-JYSDC

BOOKS 2 READ

Connecting independent readers to independent writers.